THE RECKONING

CASE FILES: POCKET-SIZED MURDER MYSTERIES

RACHEL AMPHLETT

THE RECKONING

CHAPTER ONE

The morning before the murder, a late autumn sky laden with rain clung to the rolling hills surrounding the town, the outlook oppressive and grey.

Oak and ash leaves turned from burnt orange to shades of ochre and yellow, littering the pitted asphalt surface of the driveway. They fluttered on the ground in the wind, struggled to become airborne one final time and then sank, defeated by the effort, before being crushed under the wheels of a sleek black car as it braked to a standstill outside the Georgian house.

Sadie Thorp hovered at the portico of the converted manor house with one hand on the open door, the other smoothing down her shirt, the collar stiff from newness and the nursing facility's embroidered blue logo bright above her left breast.

She finished adjusting her short ponytail, peered at the rear smoked-glass windows of the car, and wondered if its passenger was staring back at her.

A moment passed, the *tick tick* of the engine cooling the only sound until a song thrush burst from the ivy that wound its way up and over the portico, shattering the peace.

The driver's door opened and a uniformed man in his early fifties climbed out.

He had all the bearing of an ex-military man, straightening his navy jacket before moving to the rear and opening the door, his close-cropped hair unaffected by the stiff breeze.

He paused and peered over his shoulder as Sadie called out.

"Mrs Price, it's lovely to see you," she said, biting back confusion, "but I didn't think we were expecting you until four o'clock?"

A gloved hand emerged from the gloom of the vehicle, accepting the chauffeur's grip.

"Then you are mistaken."

Sadie swallowed, then fixed a smile on her face.

The smile that Helen, her manager, used

when faced with one of their more difficult residents.

And Evelyn Price promised to be one of those, she was in no doubt.

The ex-Forces' sweetheart glared at her over a pair of pink-framed glasses perching on the end of her veined nose, then raised a painted eyebrow.

The effect did nothing to hide the deep wrinkles or rheumy eyes.

"Welcome to Orchard Skilled Nursing Facility," said Sadie. "I'm sure you'll be very comfortable here."

"I should hope so, given the fees." Evelyn peeled the gloves from her hands and smacked them against her palm as she watched the driver remove her suitcases from the back of the car. "Don't put those on the ground, they'll get dirty. Straight into the house with them, Duncan."

"Certainly, Mrs Price."

Evelyn watched him for a moment, then turned to Sadie. "Are you going to stand there all day gaping, or are you going to show me to my room?"

"I – of course. Come this way, please."

She stood to one side to let the woman cross the threshold, noting how Evelyn paused in the middle of the reception area and turned full circle, her gaze lingering on the oil paintings that adorned one oak-panelled wall before she pointed at the blinking red light above a camera fixed above the front door.

"Do you get much trouble here?" she said.

"What? Sorry, no – those are just for our security while we're working on reception." Sadie gave a small shrug. "It's a health and safety requirement, that's all. We're quite a distance from the main road, and we're often working in here on our own."

Evelyn huffed under her breath in response, and Sadie hurried to the reception desk.

"There's just some paperwork to be signed before I show you to your room," she explained, hearing the note of apology in her voice.

Evelyn shot her a horrified look and took a step back. "Give that to Duncan. He deals with that sort of thing, not me."

"Here, let me." The chauffeur held out his hand and ran his gaze over the forms. "Everything will be billed to the company as requested?"

Sadie handed him the black biro from her shirt pocket. "That's right. We only have a post office box number in London for the address…"

"That'll do." He scrawled his signature beside the two crosses Helen had pencilled in the correct places on the waiver and billing agreements.

"Thank you." Sadie crossed to the reception desk, opened the bottom drawer and dropped the folder inside before locking it. She gestured to the hallway leading off to the left. "If you'd like to follow me, the lift to the first floor is this way."

"I beg your pardon, young lady, but there happens to be a perfectly good staircase over here," said Evelyn, jutting out her chin. "I didn't get to my age through lack of exercise."

"Of course… I didn't mean…" Sadie looked to the chauffeur for help.

"Mrs Price is exceptionally fit for a lady of her age," he said.

"Even so, will you be all right with the suitcases?"

"Not a bother. I'll take these up now and then I'll be off."

"Thanks. It's room number four – up the stairs, last one on the right."

"I hope it's got a garden view," said Evelyn, beady eyes watching as Duncan lifted her luggage and made his way up the stairs without a backwards glance. "We did request a garden view."

"Your room has a beautiful outlook," said Sadie, wishing she sounded less flustered and glad that Helen wasn't around to observe her embarrassment. "I'm told it's the best room in the house."

"I should think so. Not the cheapest place to stay, is it?"

Sadie took a deep breath as the chauffeur returned empty-handed at the top of the stairs, his gait nonchalant as he descended.

"Shall we go up, Mrs Price?"

"If I must."

The ninety-six-year-old adjusted her handbag strap across her forearm, then replaced her gloves and reached out for the smooth wooden bannister, determination in her eyes.

"I'll see you tomorrow afternoon as arranged, Mrs Price," said Duncan. He turned to Sadie and lowered his voice. "Don't worry. She'll be all right once she's settled."

Sadie exhaled and forced a smile. "I'm sure we'll get along fine."

CHAPTER TWO

A WIZENED HAND dropped the net curtain into place, a bronchial cough hacking its way from the man's lungs as he shuffled across to an overstuffed armchair and sank into it with a groan.

Reassuring warmth from the radiator under the window saturated the room, soaking the available air and capturing a whiff of body odour, cheap soap and aftershave that was fast receding under the notes of furniture polish and lemon-scented bathroom cleaner.

A single bed with metal side rails took up the length of one wall, beige blankets and allergy-free pillows plumped and ready to cushion the old man's form.

Sadie finished vacuuming, made sure the cable was well away from Alan Hendrick's feet in case he tripped, then pulled the laundry bag from its wicker bin and placed it next to the door.

A familiar rattle of tablets being tipped from a plastic pot filled the sudden silence.

This had become their routine: she would vacuum, he would watch and wait until she was done to take his heart pills, and then he would offer advice – whether required or otherwise – while she dusted and tidied.

"I have a theory."

She stamped on the button at the back of the vacuum cleaner and watched as the cable coiled away, the plug bumping across the stain-proof grey carpet before clattering into its burrow.

"A theory about what?"

"Not what, who. Her. The new gal. Evelyn."

"Do you know her?"

"Never seen her before in my life."

"How do you know her name, then?"

It was like this with Mr Hendrick. Information had to be gleaned from him piece by tiny piece, teased out of him. He loved to taunt, loved to hold on to facts and snippets of gossip like morsels of food to be shared.

"I overheard you talking earlier," he said.

"Did you now?" She smiled. "Were you eavesdropping?"

"Certainly not. You were talking loudly."

"All right, I believe you," she said. "So, what's this theory about?"

"How long is she here for?"

"Until tomorrow afternoon. Her usual carer is away and there's nobody around to look after her tonight."

"I don't think she's sick."

"What makes you say that?"

"I can tell. A person has a certain way of standing or talking when they're hurt. You can spot the weak ones. She isn't one of them."

"Well, maybe she needs to rest for other reasons." She moved to the bed and tucked a stray corner of the soft wool blanket under the mattress. "Convalescing can be for anything, can't it?"

"You don't know why she's here?"

"Now, Mr Hendrick – you know I can't tell you."

"Well, what *do* you know about her? There must be something you can tell me to alleviate the inordinate boredom around here."

"She sang for the troops during the war.'

"The British, you mean." Hendrick wrinkled his nose as he placed the bottle of pills on a small wooden table beside his armchair. "I didn't hear her."

"Too busy blowing up Russian tanks?"

"Did I tell you about that?"

"You did, along with the story about the man who helped you steal the German Kommandant's goat."

"It was a horrible goat. Worst I've ever tasted. Mind you, my friends in the Hungarian Resistance didn't go hungry that week, at least. Did I tell you about the time…"

Sadie tuned out his words as she sprayed a liberal amount of furniture polish onto a duster and began cleaning the mahogany-framed mirror next to the door. She had only worked at the convalescent home for four weeks but knew all of Hendrick's stories by heart.

Alan Hendrick, once known as Bertalan Hendrich. Hungarian by birth, English by circumstances these past seventy-five years. Sharp as a pin, with a twinkle in his eye.

She ran her gaze over the faded photographs in the silver frames on the windowsill of the wife who had died eight years ago and the two sons who never visited, her heart heavy with pity for the animated man she cared for.

He extracted a pocket watch and glared at the clock on the wall. "It's two minutes slow."

"Are you sure?"

"This never lies. Quality workmanship, you see. Made in the 1920s, wound daily, dropped once – and still manages to tell the right time." He jabbed a shrivelled finger at the offending digital counterpart. "That, on the other hand, is cheap, poor quality, and—"

"Okay, I'll change it."

Sadie tugged the clock from its picture hook and toggled the switch that marked the seconds before replacing it. That done, she moved around the room, dusting the arrangement of mementoes the old man had collected on a shelf beside the bathroom door as she hummed under her breath.

"Mind the crystal."

"I will." She picked up the nearest piece, the green and blue stemmed glass catching the light from the table lamp next to his armchair. "It's beautiful."

"It's Überfang. No two are the same." His voice held a sense of wonder as she turned the glass in her hand.

"Was it a gift?"

"Of sorts." Hendrick shuffled against the cushions, his eyes shifting to the window.

Sadie replaced the glass, wiped a smudge

of dust away from the corner of the shelf, and turned back to him. "Was it from when you were in the Resistance?"

"Yes." He waved his hand in front of his face as if to chase away the memories. "A long time ago now."

He was tiring.

She could hear it in his voice, see it in the way his eyelids fluttered.

It was often the case after he took his medication.

She pulled the vacuum cleaner towards the door and shoved the furniture polish and dusting cloth into the front pocket of her protective apron.

"Are you warm enough? Do you want me to turn up the heating in here?"

"No. I'm fine, dear. Are you working tonight?"

"I'm on call, yes."

"That's a shame. You should try the Palinka sometime," he said. He pointed to a dusty bottle on the shelf next to the glassware, then winked. "It will, as you youngsters say, knock your socks off."

Sadie laughed, stooping to pick up the laundry bag.

"I'll pass, thank you, Mr Hendrick. I have another room to clean yet."

CHAPTER THREE

A SUBDUED QUIETNESS filled the old house as Sadie closed the door to room number three and paused on the landing.

An eighty-year-old by the name of Roger Sanders occupied number two, and as Sadie raised her hand to knock, she heard soft snores emanating through the woodwork.

She checked her watch, the dial glinting under the soft hues of the spotlights in the ceiling.

Mr Sanders was known for his afternoon siestas, which had a habit of playing havoc with the cleaning schedule from time to time.

No matter – she would try to return later if time allowed.

Opening a covered hatch beside a fire exit, she swung the laundry bag down the metal chute, then glanced over her shoulder at the faint sound of music.

The distant notes of a swing band filtered from further along the carpeted corridor, the song a reminder of dancing around in her grandmother's kitchen while she listened to stories about rations and air raids.

Sure that the music came from Evelyn Price's room, she peered at the roster of tasks on her clipboard and noted it was almost time to change the woman's dressings.

She rolled her shoulders, heard a satisfied *crick* as a muscle relaxed, and pulled the vacuum cleaner along to the store cupboard, humming under her breath as she collected disposable gloves and a fresh crepe bandage.

Knocking once before turning her key in the lock for number four, she smiled as the music ended and the familiar crack and hiss of a well-worn vinyl record filled the silence.

"Excuse me, Mrs Price. It's time for me to change the dressing on your ankle."

The nonagenarian stood next to the smaller of the two suitcases the chauffeur had brought in from the car, the open lid exposing a miniature record player with built-in speakers. She held a dull green paper record sleeve in her hand.

"I thought you were coming in here to tell me to keep the noise down," she said, lifting the needle from the vinyl.

Sadie put down her clipboard beside a half-full water jug. "Not at all – I like it actually. It reminds me of my grandmother. She used to play that sort of music all the time. I think it reminded her of dancing with my grandfather when they first met."

"Are they both gone now?"

"My grandfather died before I was born, and I lost my grandmother about ten years ago."

"It catches up with us all eventually." Evelyn tucked the record into its sleeve, slipped it into a pocket next to the deck and then wandered over to the solitary armchair beside the window. "Did your grandmother play my songs to you?"

Sadie shook her head. "I'm sorry, Mrs Price. I haven't heard any of your songs."

"Well, I suppose you are a bit on the young side." The old woman sighed. "And you can call me Evelyn. Mrs Price makes me feel even older."

"Thank you." Snapping on the protective gloves, she crouched next to the woman and gently lifted her foot into her lap, setting the new bandage to one side. "What sort of songs did you used to sing?"

"I never had any of my own – I was too young. The songwriters were busy with the likes of Doris and Vera. I sang some of theirs and the other popular ones." Her eyes gleamed. "Occasionally I sang some of the bawdier songs that were around. It depended on the audience. Anything to take the soldiers' minds off what was going on around them for a little while."

Sadie smiled. "You must have had such a time of it. Do you still sing?"

"Oh, just for the usual anniversaries. I seem to get rolled out for all of them – the Diamond Jubilee, D-Day, VE Day. Any excuse, and off we go again."

"Do you enjoy it?"

"It's such a bother these days." Evelyn scowled. "All the security arrangements and waiting around while they check this, check that. It's different now."

"I suppose it has to be. It's all for the right reasons, isn't it?"

The woman wrinkled her nose. "So they tell me, although if they saw what we got up to back then... I used to get sent over to Belgium, France, wherever else they needed me back in the day. Flak in the skies, anti-aircraft guns on the ground…"

"It must've been dangerous."

"It was." A smile flitted across the woman's face for a moment.

"Helen, my manager, said that she'd heard you did some acting as well."

"I was always a good actress." Evelyn peered into the encroaching darkness beyond the window. "I loved that more than the singing."

"Were you in any films?"

"None that you would have heard of, no."

Sadie dropped her gaze to the woman's ankle as the last remnants of dressing loosened, and gasped at the purple-yellow bruising that dappled her skin. "What on earth did you do to yourself?"

"I'm ninety-six, young lady." Evelyn's mouth twisted. "I forget I don't move as quickly as I used to. Turned my ankle, that's all."

"This is a nasty cut."

"Hence why they're insisting I rest. Not serious enough for the hospital, but they don't trust me to be left at home on my own."

"No family?" A silence stretched out as she wound a fresh dressing around the woman's ankle, and Sadie bit her lip. "I'm sorry. I shouldn't ask."

A sigh tickled her hair as she worked, head bowed.

"I don't have any family, no. People like Duncan are the closest I have to family now."

CHAPTER FOUR

A LINGERING aroma of roast chicken dinner and steamed vegetables filled the residents' dining room.

Plates clattered in a sink, the noise echoing through the door from the kitchen while Sadie wiped down tables, shuffled chairs and cleared away the last of the unused cutlery.

She glanced up as Helen bustled into view, a clipboard in her hand while she ran through a checklist of items and worked her way around the room.

"How's our newest temporary resident getting on?" she said. "Settling in all right?"

"Evelyn? Fine, I think. Nasty cut on her ankle."

"Apparently she tripped and fell." Helen scratched her pen across the checklist, then tossed the clipboard onto the nearest table. "Right, that's that done."

Sadie gathered the last of the cutlery into her fist. "She hasn't got any family to look after her. A bit sad, given all she's done over the years for veterans."

Helen lowered her voice. "According to the woman who phoned to make the booking, Evelyn's husband died at the beginning of the war when they were both in their early twenties. She never remarried – she put all her effort into entertaining the troops around Europe and then once that was over, she got involved with different charities. Travelled all over the world as an ambassador for one of the big ones."

"Evelyn said people like her driver are like her family. Seems surprising, given how frosty we were told she could be. She's been all right with me once we got over the initial introductions this morning."

"She spoke highly of you earlier when I popped in to say hello."

"Did she?"

"Says you have good taste in music."

"She was playing some of the records my grandmother used to have. It brought back memories."

Helen opened the top drawer of a

mahogany side cupboard that ran half the length of the dining room wall as Sadie wandered over with the clean knives and forks. "I'm impressed with the way you build up a rapport with the residents."

Sadie smiled. "It's funny – I always thought I wanted to work in accident and emergency when I first started studying to be a nurse, but this seems so much more… satisfying."

"It takes a certain kind. Speaking of which – I heard Alan Hendrick was chatting you up earlier."

"I enjoy listening to him. He was a hero, wasn't he? Working with the Resistance and all that."

"A hero with an overactive imagination," said Helen, not unkindly. "I'm not sure how many of those escapades were his or someone else's."

"Still, if it wasn't for people like him—"

"Help!"

Sadie jumped at the shout from the residents' lounge, took one look at Helen's face, and ran towards the noise.

When she entered the room, Alan Hendrick was sitting in one of the chairs facing the television, his hands splayed on each of the arms, his face stricken.

Roger Sanders was leaning over his walking frame towards Hendrick, his face puce with rage as he shook a fist at him.

"You stole it," he snarled. "It is not yours."

He held up a gold pocket watch and swung it on its chain, then slipped it into the pocket of his cardigan.

Hendrick's eyes found Sadie's, his expression pleading as she and Helen hurried to his side.

"Don't be ridiculous, Sanders," he pleaded. "You've completely lost the plot. Give it back – it's mine."

"Now, now, gentlemen." Helen rested her hand on Sanders' arm. "Roger, did you remember to take your tablets this afternoon?"

Sanders shoved his hands into his cardigan pockets and lowered his chin. "I don't remember."

"All right, let's have a look at this watch."

Helen held out her hand, her voice calm as if she was dealing with a pair of bickering teenagers instead of two old men.

Sanders withdrew it from his pocket, his mouth downturned. "It's mine."

Turning over the watch between her fingers, Helen's gaze slipped to Hendrick then back. "Mr Sanders, I'm sorry but I think you're wrong. I've seen Mr Hendrick using this watch on many occasions – before you lived here, too. I believe the watch is his."

Tears formed in the old man's eyes, and Sadie looked away for a moment, embarrassed for him.

"I don't remember," he managed. "I don't remember anything anymore."

Helen placed the watch on a low table beside Hendrick's chair and sighed. "Well, I'm sure we can put this all behind us. There's no harm done, after all. Shall we get you upstairs, Mr Sanders? I'll fetch you a cup of tea."

She pulled Sadie to one side and lowered her voice as they watched Sanders shuffle away, the man stabbing his walking frame into the carpet before each tentative step. "He'll be fine once I've got him settled and checked his medication. Help Mr Hendrick back to his room, then take your break. With Anna off sick, I'll need you to take turns with me to run the night shift so get your head down for a couple of hours. I'll wake you when it's time to swap over."

"All right, thanks."

The creak of the walking frame retreated into the corridor as Helen guided Mr Sanders away from the dining room, and then Sadie wandered across to Hendrick.

"Would you like me to bring you a warm drink?"

"No, that's fine. Thank you. I think I'll go to bed now. This whole episode has left me quite exhausted." He leaned on his walking stick and eased himself away from the soft cushions, nodding as she cradled his elbow in her palm while he found his balance.

"Don't forget this." Evelyn crossed the carpet, her face pale as she handed over the watch to Hendrick, her gaze roaming his face while he turned the watch in his hands. "That's quite a specimen. How long have you had it?"

"It was a gift – from a long time ago," he said, dropping it into his pocket. He turned to Sadie. "I suppose you want to come with me to make sure I don't get into any more trouble."

"Are you going to be all right, Mr Hendrick?" she said as she opened the door to his room and switched on a lamp that gave out a soft glow from its position on the bedside table.

"I suppose so." He shrugged off his worn jacket, mumbling his thanks as she shook it out and placed it on a coat hanger ready for the morning. He lowered himself to the armchair beside the window as she drew the curtains, his nose wrinkling. "It isn't the first time he's threatened me, you know."

"Really?" Sadie couldn't help the surprise in her voice. "Why on earth would he do that?"

"It's either his dementia or the tablets he's taking."

"That's awful."

As she tucked a blanket around his legs and helped him put on his suede slippers, Hendrick managed a smile and held up his walking stick.

"Don't worry, petal. If he tries anything again, I'll whack him with this. That'll teach him."

"I'd much rather you pulled the emergency cord, Mr Hendrick. Good night."

CHAPTER FIVE

A COMFORTING GLOOM had descended on the office by ten-thirty and, after a taking a break as Helen had suggested, Sadie was content to work in the warm light from her desk lamp that counteracted the glare from her computer screen.

She signed out of her personal email account, closed the window, and returned to the health and safety report she was typing up for Helen in relation to the altercation between Hendrick and Sanders.

Eyeing the growing amount of paperwork stacked in the tray beside the screen, she resolved to take care of the filing first thing tomorrow. The metal cabinet drawers that lined the wall behind her chair tended to rattle and scrape, and it would do no good if the residents complained about the noise while they were trying to sleep.

Humming under her breath, the memory of her grandmother still fresh in her mind, she rubbed at tired eyes and reached out for the mug of coffee next to her keyboard.

When she'd seen the job advertised at the nursing facility, she had approached it as a stepping stone – a way to gain some work experience to lend weight to the paper qualifications that sat in her personnel file in another locked cabinet under the windowsill to her left.

However, only a few weeks into the role, she could understand why people chose this as a vocation. Some of their residents were only short-term visitors, like Evelyn Price, but others had nowhere else to go. It seemed to her a harsh reality that in their time of need and despite what many of them had done for their country during the war and afterwards, they had been discarded by society.

People like her and her colleagues kept them safe from the harsh world beyond the ornate gardens of the nursing facility.

She pulled up the sleeves of her sweater, wondering if she should turn the thermostat down the next time she conducted her walk through the silent building. It was a fine balance between keeping their guests comfortable and not melting while on the job.

Putting the coffee aside, she exhaled and vowed to finish the report before eleven o'clock and the rostered changeover. At least that way, Helen could read through it when they switched.

She reached into her bag and pulled out a muesli bar, a small snack to keep her going until it was her turn to head upstairs to the twin room she shared with her manager.

It was a simple set-up – whoever was rostered for the night shifts shared a room on the second floor, away from the reception area in order that a few hours' sleep could be taken in between keeping an eye on the residents and catching up with the administrative work.

Working four days in a row at a time, Sadie had become adept at packing the small suitcase she used for work. When she had first started, she had rather optimistically placed a paperback book inside – the reality was, the moment her head hit the pillow, she was asleep until her alarm went off the next morning.

She raised her head as a red flashing light appeared on a panel above the computer screen.

There was no warning, no audible siren, but the light meant that Alan Hendrick had pulled the emergency cord in his room.

Checking that her set of master keys was clipped to her belt, Sadie snatched up the mobile first-aid kit next to the office door and raced towards the stairs, her footsteps muted by the carpeted treads.

When she reached the landing to the first floor, Evelyn and another resident – Mrs Taylor – were standing outside their doors, their faces bewildered.

"I heard a crash," said Mrs Taylor, her voice trembling.

"Excuse me, ladies." Sadie didn't wait for their response, brushed past them and inserted her key into the lock on Hendrick's door. "Mr Hendrick – Alan – is everything okay?"

A crumpled form sat against the nearest bed leg, and as Sadie reached out to her left and slapped the light switch, she blinked before dropping to the floor.

Alan Hendrik looked up at her, his eyes bewildered, the red emergency cord tangled around his fingers.

"There was somebody in my room."

Sadie peered at the window, but the

curtains were still drawn closed and no wind billowed the material away from the glass.

"Let me take a look at you. Did you fall out of bed? Are you hurt anywhere?"

"I'm fine," he snapped. "I stumbled over the corner of the blanket when I got up to see who it was. I must've been half asleep and tripped."

"There was no-one else here when I came in, Mr Hendrick."

"There was someone here, I tell you!"

"The door was locked," said Sadie, keeping her voice calm. "No-one's been in here. I've got the only other key."

"What if someone took your key? What if someone got into the house when you weren't looking?"

"I can assure you, all the doors downstairs are locked as well – and if someone had come to the front door, I'd have seen them on the cameras, wouldn't I?"

"I'll bet it was that bloody Sanders. Wanting to steal my things." His eyes drifted to the wooden shelf and the Überfang glassware before finding her once more. "He's mad, you know."

"He's got early-stage dementia, Mr Hendrick, that's all." Sadie bent over, wrapped her arms under the old man's and coaxed him upright. "Let's get you back into bed before you catch a cold."

Hendrick wilted in her arms as she pivoted and sat him on the bed, the mattress sagging a little.

"Maybe I *was* dreaming," he murmured.

"It must have been very vivid, to frighten you like that."

"I wasn't frightened." His chin jutted out. "I was angry."

At that moment Sanders appeared at the open door, his hair ruffled, pillow lines across one cheek.

"What the bloody hell is going on?" he asked, sleep coating his words with a bleariness that matched his eyes. "What's all the noise about?"

"Mr Hendrick called out in his sleep, that's all," said Sadie, turning her attention back to Hendrick and helping him under the covers. "It's nothing – best go back to your room, Mr Sanders."

"Hmmph." Sanders tightened the belt of his dressing-gown, then shuffled his walking frame around. "Probably dreaming up more stories about his time in the Resistance."

Hendrick pushed Sadie's hand away and leaned forward.

"I'll have you know—"

"Leave him," said Sadie. "You know what he can be like. You need to rest."

Leaving the bedside light on and making sure Hendrick had a fresh glass of water within easy reach, she said goodnight and closed the door.

The lock slid into place with a smooth click and after clipping the keyring to her belt, she closed her eyes a moment, wondering if she would get any sleep herself tonight after the fright Hendrick had just given her.

She jumped as a hand wrapped around her forearm and turned to see Evelyn staring at her, her eyes wide.

"Did he say Hendrick was in the Resistance?"

"Yes. Hungary, apparently. He says he saved a lot of lives."

Evelyn shook her head, her face crestfallen. Her grip loosened on Sadie's arm before she turned and wandered back towards her room, leaving a trailing scent of lavender in her wake, her shaking voice barely above a whisper.

"The stories we could tell…."

CHAPTER SIX

SADIE TUGGED the brush through her thick brown hair, snapped an elastic band over the ends and fastened her wristwatch as she paced the small staff bedroom she shared with Helen.

Bright sunshine sparkled through the window that overlooked the car park and delivery entrance to the kitchen, and she watched as a cheeky sparrow perched on the sill a moment before it plucked a bug from the wisteria branches that twisted across the brickwork beside the glass and flew away.

Placing her shower gel and hair straighteners into the locker by the side of the single bed she used while on night shifts, she pocketed the key and reached for the door handle before snatching her hand away as it opened.

"Oh."

"Sorry – I was hoping to catch you before you came downstairs." Helen waved her back inside and pulled the door closed.

"What's wrong?"

"Alan Hendrick passed away in his sleep last night."

"What—"

"The local doctor's in his room now, and two people from the funeral home have just turned up." Helen raised her hands. "Hell of a way to start the day, I know, but…"

"When did you find out?" Sadie sat on the end of her bed, trembling.

"About an hour ago when he didn't show up for breakfast. Rosie's on reception this morning, and went up to find him." Her shoulders sagged. "He was in his armchair, next to the window."

Sadie sniffed, then pulled out a paper tissue from her trouser pocket and blew her nose. "He loved to sit by the window and watch the garden. Do you think… do you think he knew?"

Helen gave her a sad smile. "Perhaps. He looks very peaceful. Would you like to come and say goodbye to him?"

"Is – is that all right?"

"He always said how much he loved

chatting with you." Helen held out her hand. "Come on. I'll go with you. The doctor's just doing the paperwork so they can take his body away."

Sadie fell into step beside her as they wandered downstairs to the first floor and along to room number three, her thoughts tumbling.

She'd seen a few dead bodies during her training, but this was different; more personal. Helen was right – he'd enjoyed her time with Hendrick and his anecdotes, however far-fetched they might have been.

"I'm going to miss him."

"We all are."

The door to number three was ajar, and the muffled and reverent voices spilling out through the gap fell silent as the two women entered.

Helen was right – Alan Hendrick did look peaceful, his head tilted to one side and his eyes closed.

The doctor had placed Hendrick's hands in his lap, and as Sadie wandered across to where his still form sat in the armchair, she reached out and touched his fingers.

"I'm going to miss you, Alan. And your stories."

"The paperwork's done," said the doctor,

turning his attention to Helen. "I'm happy for these two to take him now."

"Thank you." Helen's voice floated across to where Sadie crouched, and she straightened as her supervisor gestured to the older of the two men from the funeral parlour. "Would you like to get him ready?"

Sadie stood to one side as the men unfolded a stretcher and gently lifted Hendrick onto it.

The younger man paused at Hendrick's shoulder, his head bowed a moment before he held out a chain to Helen.

"There's a key on this. Might be for the bureau over there, or something."

"Thanks. I'll take a look after he's gone so we can make a list of everything."

The man nodded and then draped a blanket over Hendrick before positioning himself to lift his end of the stretcher.

Sadie opened the door and stepped across the threshold to make way for them. When she glanced over her shoulder, she was astounded to see the other residents from the first floor standing next to the stairs, their heads bowed.

Crossing the landing, she peered over the stair bannister to see the kitchen staff, cleaners and other nurses had done the same, forming an honour guard down the stairs and all the way to the front door.

Helen joined her. "It's our way of showing our respect on their final journey."

"It's lovely." Sadie fell into place beside her supervisor as the two funeral parlour workers passed, the stretcher carrying Alan Hendrick's covered form borne between them as if it weighed little more than paper.

She wiped a tear from her eye as they continued down the stairs, recalling how delicate she'd thought the man as she'd helped him to his feet the night before.

"How about cracking open that Palinka he was always going on about and raising a toast?" Roger Sanders leaned over his walker and leered at the receding figures as they passed from sight.

"That's not appropriate, Mr Sanders, as well you know," Helen scolded him. "Now, isn't it time for your medication?"

He grumbled under his breath but acquiesced as one of the day nurses reached the top of the stairs and advanced towards him.

With that the other residents departed, retreating to the privacy of their respective rooms.

Sadie noticed Evelyn lingered on the

landing a moment longer, and then the woman gave her a slight nod and turned away.

When she too had gone back to her room, Sadie caught up with Helen.

"What if that altercation with Sanders last night caused Mr Hendrick's heart to fail?"

"I don't think so. The doctor said he showed no sign of stress. Besides, Alan was quite a robust character despite his heart condition." She exhaled, then gestured down the stairs. "Go on – the dining room needs to be cleared up now breakfast is finished down there, and you'll have to get Mrs Price ready to be collected at one o'clock this afternoon while I make a start going through Alan's things and cataloguing them."

"Life goes on," Sadie murmured.

CHAPTER SEVEN

SADIE KEPT a watchful eye on Roger Sanders as he accompanied his daughter around the concrete path that bisected the landscaped gardens beyond the house.

She shivered, peering up at the grey clouds that shrouded the horizon, threatening rain.

Zipping up the black quilted coat she wore over her uniform, she sniffed the air. At the far end of the lawn, the contracted landscape gardener had started a small bonfire to cope with all the leaves he had raked from the paths around the property.

It would do no good at all if one of their residents slipped and fell.

"We'll be off now."

Duncan's voice jolted Sadie from her daydreaming, and she turned to see him on the threshold, Evelyn's arm looped through his as she left the reception area.

The chauffeur had already carried the two suitcases downstairs and placed them in the car, the portable record player treated with particular reverence.

"Wait here a moment, Mrs Price," he said. "I'll get the door open first."

"I hope you found everything all right during your stay…" said Sadie, the words dying on her lips. "I'm sorry. I realise this morning has been traumatic."

The older woman moved to where she stood beyond the portico.

"It was simply Mr Hendrick's time." Evelyn looked up at the Georgian façade, her eyes wistful.

"I suppose so. That's what Helen said earlier." Sadie offered her arm and walked side by side with the woman to the car, nodding to Duncan as he opened the back door. "I hope your recovery continues to go well, Mrs Price."

"I'm sure it will. I have a few more appointments to keep, but I'm determined to make every one of them count."

Evelyn turned and rested her hand on Duncan's outstretched arm before lowering herself onto the back seat.

The chauffeur made sure she was comfortable, then closed the door and faced Sadie, shaking his head.

"An amazing woman," he said, his voice full of awe. "Hard to believe she's in her nineties now. Rumour has it she worked for SOE during the war."

"SOE?"

"Secret Service."

"But I thought she sang. She said she used to entertain the troops. And act."

"Oh, she was an actress all right. God knows what she got up to behind enemy lines. They've never done an official count of how many lives she saved. Or killed."

Sadie blinked, aware that her mouth had dropped open.

The back door to the car opened, a leathery forearm visible in the gap between the hand rest and the darkened interior.

"Duncan? It's time to go. Hurry, or else I shall be late for my next appointment."

The chauffeur shot Sadie a rueful smile as the door slammed shut. "You heard her. We'll be off. Thanks for making her stay comfortable."

Sadie spun on her heel and raced through the front door, up the stairs.

She found Helen in Alan Hendrick's room,

standing by the window while she held a faded photograph up to the light.

"I found out who Evelyn was, what she did," she blurted.

Her supervisor said nothing for a moment and instead turned the photograph around in a shaking hand. "Hendrick wasn't who he said he was, either."

"What?"

The image was yellowed with age.

In the background, a high wire fence was secured into place with concrete posts. Behind the wire, skeletal people wearing dirty striped shirts and matching trousers stared at the photographer, their expressions conveying despair, starvation, horror.

In front of the wire fence, Alan Hendrick stood stock-still, his spine rigid.

Sadie's eyes took in the black uniform, the polished calf-high boots, the skull and crossbones cap badge.

He held up a pocket watch on a chain, dangling it so that the light caught the gold casing.

Even with the passing of time, she recognised it.

"Where did you find this?" Sadie took the photograph, afraid that Helen would drop the frame, and stared at the image.

"Locked away in the bureau. There's more," said Helen. "Diaries. Lists. Medals he was given by Hitler."

Bile rose in Sadie's throat as she stared at the young man in uniform.

She raised her gaze to the crystal antiques that lined the shelf and then her eyes fell to the pocket watch on the bedside table, its dials frozen in time.

"He didn't steal the Kommandant's goat, did he?" she managed. "He *was* the Kommandant. He took all of these trinkets from those poor people."

"What do we do?"

"I think it's already been done," said Sadie, dropping the photograph onto the armchair beside the window.

She raised her gaze to the panes in time to see the black car passing the manicured lawn and rhododendron bushes that lined the driveway, the licence plate obscured by billowing smoke from the gardener's bonfire.

Its brake lights flashed once when it reached the gateposts, and then Evelyn Price was gone.

"If that's your name," Sadie whispered.

THE END

ABOUT THE AUTHOR

Rachel Amphlett is a USA Today bestselling author of crime fiction and spy thrillers, many of which have been translated worldwide.

Her novels are available in eBook, print, and audiobook formats from libraries and retailers as well as her website shop.

A keen traveller, Rachel has both Australian and British citizenship.

Find out more about Rachel's books at: www.rachelamphlett.com.

www.ingramcontent.com/pod-product-compliance
Lightning Source LLC
Chambersburg PA
CBHW030846200726
48285CB00007B/2573